The Bear Hug

Sean Callahan

Illustrated by Laura J. Bryant

www.av2books.com

Your AV² Media Enhanced book gives you a fiction readalong online. Log on to www.av2books.com and enter the unique book code from this page to use your readalong.

AV² Readalong Navigation

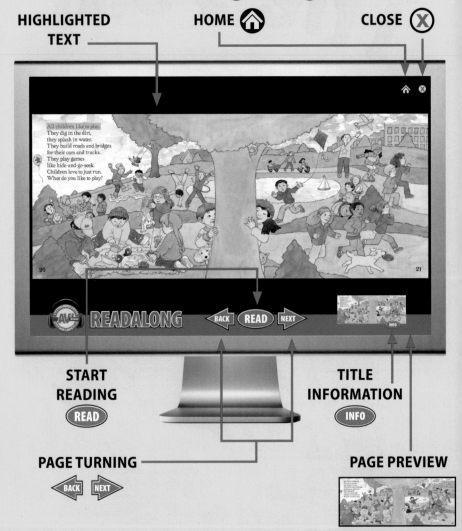

HIGHLIGHTED TEXT

HOME

CLOSE

START READING — READ

PAGE TURNING — BACK NEXT

TITLE INFORMATION — INFO

PAGE PREVIEW

Go to **www.av2books.com**, and enter this book's unique code.

BOOK CODE

L266293

AV² by Weigl brings you media enhanced books that support active learning.

First Published by

ALBERT WHITMAN & COMPANY
Publishing children's books since 1919

Published by AV² by Weigl
350 5th Avenue, 59th Floor New York, NY 10118
Websites: www.av2books.com   www.weigl.com

Printed in the United States of America in Brainerd, Minnesota

1 2 3 4 5 6 7 8 9 0   19 18 17 16 15

042015
WEP021715

Library of Congress Cataloging-in-Publication Data

Callahan, Sean, 1965-
  The bear hug / Sean Callahan.
    pages cm. -- (Av2 fiction readalong)
  Summary: Cubby loves spending time with Grandpa Bear, especially when Grandpa gives him the Bear Hug.
  ISBN 978-1-4896-3852-6 (hard cover : alk. paper) -- ISBN 978-1-4896-3853-3 (single user ebook) -- ISBN 978-1-4896-3854-0 (multi-user ebook)
  [1. Grandparent and child--Fiction. 2. Bears--Fiction. 3. Hugging--Fiction.] I. Title.
  PZ7.C12974Bea 2015
  [E]--dc23
                                      2014050031

Text copyright ©2006 by Sean Francis Callahan.
Illustrations copyright ©2006 by Laura J. Bryant.
Published in 2006 by Albert Whitman & Company.

For Sophie, Charlotte, and Uncle Jerry—S.C.

To Nana and Grand Pop—L.J.B.

Every Sunday, Cubby walked to Grandpa Bear's house. "Hi, Grandpa Bear," Cubby said.

Grandpa Bear taught little Cubby
how to be a bear.
They always worked on
their growling.

"Grrrrroooowwwllll!"

In the spring, Grandpa Bear
showed off his fishing technique.
"It's all in the wrist,"
Grandpa Bear said.

On summer days, they
splashed at the swimming hole.

"Look out
belooooooooooow!"
Grandpa bellowed.

In the fall, they hunted for food wherever they could find it.
"Thanks for the bear claw, Grandpa," Cubby said.

In the winter, Grandpa Bear
showed Cubby how to hibernate.

"Zzzzzzzzzzzzzzzzzzzzzzzzzzzz."

On rainy days, they looked at snapshots of when Grandpa Bear was a cub.

"Wow, that's your grandpa giving *you* the Bear Hug," Cubby said.

The Bear Hug!

Cubby loved the Bear Hug.
It was the best thing about going
to Grandpa Bear's.
"Nobody *ever* gets out of
the Bear Hug," Grandpa Bear
warned Cubby.
"I'm going to get out,"
Cubby vowed.

"Do you give up?" Grandpa Bear asked.
"No," Cubby said. "I'm gonna

wiggle, wiggle, wiggle

my way out!"

"Do you give up?" Grandpa Bear yelled.
"No," Cubby said. "I'm gonna

wriggle, wriggle, wriggle

my way out!"

"Do you give up *now*?" whispered Grandpa.
"No!" Cubby said with a shout. "I'm gonna

giggle,
giggle,
giggle—
'cause I'm
OUT!"

Grandpa Bear moaned. "You got out of the Bear Hug! How'd you do it?"

"Same way as last week," Cubby said. "There's really nothing to it!"